Gamer Boy

Ready, Freddy!

2nd Grade

by ABBY KLEIN

illustrated by
JOHN McKINLEY

Scholastic Inc.

To Joel,
My one and only Game Boy!
Love you forever . . .
Love,
A.K.

CHAPTERS

I have a problem. A really, really big problem. I got the best new video game, *Wonder World*, and now I want to play it all the time. I have to get to level ten before any of my friends.

Let me tell you about it.

CHAPTER 1

Ants on a Log

The school bus stopped in front of my house. I jumped out followed by my two best friends, Josh and Robbie, and we ran inside.

"Mom, where are you?" I called.

"I'm in the kitchen, Freddy!"

We dashed into the kitchen and dropped our backpacks on the floor.

"Hello, boys," said my mom. "How was school today?"

"Pretty good," I said. "We got to play blob tag in PE, and I love that game. It's so much fun!"

"Blob tag? What's that?" asked my mom.

"Well, one person is It," I said, "and they try to tag other people."

"If you get tagged," said Robbie, "then you hold hands with the person who is It and try to tag more people."

"Every time someone gets tagged, they join hands, and the blob keeps getting bigger and bigger," said Josh.

"That does sound like a lot of fun," said my mom. "All of that running around must have made you hungry. Would you boys like a snack?"

"Yes, please!" we all said together.

"What would you like?" asked my mom.

"How about ants on a log," I said.

"EEEWWWWW!" Josh said, making a face. "You eat ants? That's disgusting!"

"Ha, ha, ha! No!" I said, laughing. "I don't eat ants!"

"But I thought you just said you wanted to eat ants on a log for a snack," said Josh.

"I did."

Josh turned to Robbie. "I don't get it. Can you please explain it to me? What is Freddy talking about?"

Robbie laughed. "Ants on a log is the name of a yummy snack. You take a piece of celery, put some peanut butter on it, and then stick some raisins on top of the peanut butter."

"Oh! I get it," said Josh. "The ants are really raisins. You scared me there for a minute. I thought you actually wanted to eat ants!"

"So do you want to try it?" I asked.

"Sure," said Josh. "As long as it's raisins and not real ants!"

"Don't worry, Josh," said my mom as she went to get our snack. "I don't let Freddy bring any creepy-crawlies into the house, and I certainly don't let him eat them!"

Josh laughed. "Good to know, Mrs. Thresher."

My mom brought the ingredients over to the kitchen table. "Here is the celery, the peanut butter, and the raisins. Would you boys like me to make it, or do you want to make it yourselves?"

"Thanks, Mom, but I think we want to make it," I said.

"All right," said my mom. "Just don't make a big mess and try not to get peanut butter all over the table."

"We won't," I said, smiling, and my mom left the room.

"So what do I have to do first?" asked Josh.

"Just watch me. Take a piece of celery, slather some peanut butter on it like this, and then

stick the raisins on top. Ta-da! Ants on a log!" I said, taking a bite. "Mmmm, mmmmm, good."

Josh and Robbie each made one. Josh took a bite. "Yum! This *is* really good, Freddy."

"I can't believe you've never had this before," said Robbie. "Freddy and I make it all the time. It's one of our favorite snacks!"

"I can see why. It's really delicious," said Josh, licking the peanut butter off his fingers.

We all made a few more to eat, licked our fingers clean, and then put everything away.

"Now what should we do?" said Robbie.

"I know!" I said. "Let's go outside and look for some real ants to put in my ant farm. Some of them escaped the other night."

"They escaped?" said Josh. "Where did they go?"

"Maybe into Suzie's bed," I said, snickering.

"You're kidding," said Robbie. "Did you really put ants in your sister's bed?"

"I told you they escaped," I said, grinning.

Josh laughed. "Wow! That must have been some crazy scene!"

Robbie shook his head. "You're lucky your mom didn't see that, or you would be in BIG trouble."

I just smiled.

"Let's get going," said Robbie. "I love bug hunting in your backyard, and it sounds like you need some more ants."

"How are we going to catch them?" asked Josh.

"I've got some bug catchers up in my tree house," I said.

The three of us ran outside and climbed up the ladder to my tree house. I looked around. "Here's one of the bug catchers," I said, tossing it to Josh.

"Good throw," he said as he reached up with one hand to catch it.

"I found another one," said Robbie, pulling it out from under a baseball glove.

"Now we just need one more for me," I said, scanning the floor. "Where could it be?"

"Found it!" Josh yelled. "It rolled under that stool," he said, pointing straight ahead.

I got down on my belly, reached under the stool, and pulled it out.

"Great! Now we're all ready to catch some ants," I said. "Let's go!"

We climbed down from the tree house and walked to the back of the yard. "This is the best place to look," I said. "I usually find a lot back here."

"Hey, look!" said Josh, laughing. "Ants on a log." He pointed to a long line of ants marching across a skinny stick.

I got down on my hands and knees in the dirt and stuck my nose right next to the stick.

"Watch out!" said Robbie. "You don't want those ants to crawl up your nose."

"That would be really gross," said Josh.

I laughed. "I'm just trying to see them up close," I said.

"Well, that's a little too close," said Josh. "Just put them in your bug catcher, and then you can hold the jar as close to your face as you want."

I lifted up the stick and gently shook the ants into my jar. I turned the jar around in my hand and studied them carefully. "This is a good start, but we're going to need a lot more," I said.

The three of us hunted around until we found enough ants to fill up all three of our bug catchers.

"Wow! This is a lot of ants," said Robbie.

"If Suzie is squirming on the bus tomorrow, I'll know she's got ants in her pants," Josh said, laughing.

We climbed back up to the tree house, carefully put the ants in my ant farm, and closed the lid.

"Now what should we do?" said Robbie.

"I know!" said Josh. "Let's play that new video game *Wonder World*. It's so awesome!"

"We can't," I mumbled.

"Why not?" said Josh.

"Because I don't have it."

"What do you mean you don't have it? Everybody has it," said Josh.

"Everybody except me," I said, sighing.

"Then you'll have to come to my house tomorrow after school, so we can play it," said Josh. "Wait until you see it. You're going to love it!"

CHAPTER 2

Wonder World

The next day after school, Robbie and I went over to Josh's house to play *Wonder World*.

"We have to go down to the basement. That's where my gaming system is set up," said Josh.

"I can't wait to play," I said. "Everyone at school keeps talking about *Wonder World*."

"That's because it's the best game ever!" said Robbie.

We went down to the basement, and Josh turned on the game. He took one of the controllers and handed the other one to Robbie. "One cool thing is you can play this game by yourself, or you can play with a split screen and play against someone else," said Josh. "Since Robbie knows how to play, we'll play first, and you can watch, Freddy."

"Okay," I said. "Good idea."

Two characters appeared. "This is me, and this is Robbie," Josh said, pointing to the screen. "The first thing we have to do is build a house."

"Why do you have to do that first?" I asked.

"Because your house is the only place you are safe from the Serpents."

"The what?" I said.

"The Evil Serpents," said Robbie.

"Why are they evil?"

"Because they have a venomous bite," said Josh, "and if they catch you, they will bite you."

"And then what happens?"

"You die, and you have to start all over again," said Josh.

"That's a real bummer," I said.

"Tell me about it," Robbie said, laughing. "It's already happened to me twice!"

"They are really sneaky," said Josh. "They come out of nowhere. You always have to be watching for them, and you have to build a strong house so they can't get in. If one starts chasing you, then you have to run back to your house as fast as you can."

"So how do you build a house?" I asked.

"You have to use your tools and chop down some trees to get wood," said Robbie.

"Tools? Where do I get the tools?" I said.

"Every player has a toolbox. You start with certain tools, but you get a new tool every time you move to the next level," said Josh.

"How do you move from one level to the next?" I asked.

"You have to find a buried treasure," said Robbie.

"There is an enchanted treasure buried somewhere at each level," said Josh. "You can't move to the next level until you find that treasure."

"Have you found any of the treasures yet?" I said.

"I found the precious ruby, the golden crown, and the mystical crystal," said Josh.

"Really? That's awesome! I've only found the precious ruby," said Robbie. "You have to find all ten treasures to win the game."

"Why do you have to have all ten of them?"

"Because in order to win the game, you have to bring the enchanted treasures to the Wonder World Palace and give them to the Wizard of Wonder World," said Josh.

"Is it hard to find the treasures?" I said.

"One of the tools in your toolbox is a metal detector," said Robbie. "So you can use that to figure out if something is buried underground."

"That seems pretty easy," I said.

"It would be if there weren't any Triglops," said Josh.

"Triglops? What are those?" I said.

"They are three-headed monsters that guard the treasures," said Josh. "They are invisible until you start digging, and then they magically appear and try to attack you."

"Really? What do you do if they attack you?" I said.

"You have to shoot them with your red laser," said Robbie. "That's the only way they disappear."

"Wow! How do you know all of this stuff?" I asked. "This game seems really complicated."

"I watched some videos online," said Josh. "You can actually watch people play the game, and they explain what they are doing as they go along."

"I did that, too," said Robbie. "That's how I learned about all of the treasures, and what to do if you are attacked by the Triglops."

"Why don't you watch us play a little bit," said Josh. "I think you'll get the hang of it."

I watched the screen carefully.

"So if you click here," said Josh, "your toolbox appears, and you can open it up. Do you see this here? This is your ax. You're going to need it to chop down some trees."

"Then you need to find a forest," said Robbie. "I think I see one over there, so I'm going to check it out."

Robbie's and Josh's characters started running toward the forest. All of a sudden, Josh's character stopped to pick some flowers.

"What are you doing?" I asked. "Robbie is going to beat you if you stop to pick flowers."

"These flowers are very important," said Josh.

"Yes, very important," said Robbie. "I can't believe you found some already. You are so lucky!"

"Why are they so important?"

"Because Ariana holds the key to the Wonder World Palace. You can't get in without the key," said Josh.

"Ariana? Who's that?"

"She's a half girl, half unicorn," said Robbie.

"But why do you need the flowers?" I asked.

"Because she won't give you the key unless you bring her a dozen rainbow flowers," said Josh.

Josh put two flowers in his pocket and ran into the forest. He took out his ax and started to chop down some trees. "You need to chop down about four trees to get enough wood for your house."

Robbie had already chopped down his trees and was racing back with his wood to build his house. "It's better if you build your house up on a mountain," said Robbie.

"Why don't you just build it near that lake?" I said. "Then it would be easy to get water."

"Because the Evil Serpents aren't very good at climbing," said Robbie.

"I built my first house right near that lake," said Josh, "and the Serpents got me right away. Then the next time, I built my house higher up, and I was able to get back inside before they reached me. I learned my lesson! Now I always build my house on a mountain."

"Good to know," I said. "I definitely have a lot to learn!"

"The best way to learn is to just play the game a lot," said Robbie.

"At first I made a lot of mistakes, but now I'm

getting better," said Josh. "I've already made it to level three."

"Level three! No way!" said Robbie.

Josh nodded and smiled.

"How many levels are there?" I asked.

"Ten," said Josh. "You have to get to level ten to enter the Queen's Palace."

Ten levels! If I was ever going to learn this game, then I was going to have to get one of my own . . . and soon!

CHAPTER 3

Pretty Please with a Cherry on Top?

That night at dinner my mom asked, "Did you have fun at Josh's house today?"

"Yes, I had a lot of fun!" I said.

"I can't believe you think looking for ants is so much fun," said my sister, Suzie.

"Who said we were looking for ants?"

"Isn't that what you were doing in our backyard yesterday?" said Suzie. "Getting more ants for your ant farm?"

"I really wish you would not go searching for

ants," said my mom. "I think some of them crawl onto your clothes, and then they accidentally end up in the house."

"I even found some in my bed the other day!" said Suzie.

"Oh my goodness!" said my mom. "Ants in your bed . . . crawling on you when you were asleep!"

"I didn't have any in my bed," I said. I had to cover my mouth, so my mom and Suzie wouldn't see me smiling.

"You know how much I hate creepy-crawly things," said my mom. "Freddy, do you have any ants crawling on you right now?"

"No, because we weren't looking for ants at Josh's house."

"Were you boys playing catch?" asked my dad. "You know Little League is starting soon."

"No, we weren't playing catch," I said. "But maybe after dinner we can throw the ball around a little bit."

"I would love to do that," said my dad.

"If you weren't looking for ants or playing catch, then what were you doing?" asked my mom.

"Playing *Wonder World*."

"*Wonder World*? What's that?" asked my dad.

"It's a new video game everyone is playing," said Suzie. "That's all kids are talking about at school."

"It is so cool," I said. "You have to build stuff, and there is buried treasure, and there's these Evil Serpents that try to catch you, and—"

"Whoa! Slow down there," said my dad. "You're talking so fast I can barely understand what you're saying. Did you just say Evil Serpents?"

I nodded. "Yep."

"What do they do?" said my mom.

"They bite, and if you get bitten by one, then you die and have to start the game all over again."

"Well, then you definitely want to stay away from those," said my mom. "They sound scary."

"What is the point of the game?" said Suzie. "Are you just trying to find a buried treasure? Because that sounds kind of dumb to me."

"No!" I said. "You're not just trying to find *one* buried treasure. You're trying to find ten enchanted treasures, so you can give them to the Wizard of Wonder World. That's how you win."

"This game sounds kind of complicated," said my dad.

"The directions on how to play must be as thick as a book!" said my mom. "It must have taken Josh and Robbie a long time to read all those directions."

"Kids don't usually learn how to play video games by reading directions," said Suzie.

"They don't?" said my mom. "Then how do they learn how to play?"

"People film themselves playing the game and explain what they are doing as they go along," said Suzie. "Then they post their videos online, and you can watch them to learn what to do."

"That's how Josh and Robbie learned how to play," I said. "Then they were trying to teach me today."

"How many levels are there?" asked Suzie.

"Ten," I said.

"Ten! That's a lot," said Suzie. "It could take forever to go through that many levels."

"Josh is already on level three, and he's only been playing for a few days," I said.

"He must be playing all the time," said my dad.

"He is! He even got up at five o'clock this morning to play before he went to school."

"Five o'clock!" said my mom. "That seems a little crazy."

"Not really," I said, "because Robbie told me that the best way to learn the game is to just play it a lot."

"And it's like a big contest at school," said Suzie. "Everyone is trying to be the first person to reach level ten. I heard kids talking about it in the lunchroom today."

"See!" I said. "I just have to get it!"

"Get what?" said my mom.

I sighed. "Haven't you been listening to anything I've been saying, Mom? I have to get *Wonder World*!"

"Can't you play it when you go over to Robbie's or Josh's house? Why do you need one of your own?" asked my mom.

"Because I have to be the first person to reach level ten, and I can only do that if I have my own *Wonder World* video game."

"How are you going to get it?" asked my dad.

That seemed like a silly question. "Buy it, of course!"

"How are you going to buy it?"

"Is this a trick question?" I said. "With money. Isn't that how you buy things . . . with money?"

"How much is it?" asked my mom.

"I think it's thirty dollars."

"Thirty dollars! That seems like a lot of money for a silly game," said my mom.

"It's not silly. It's the best game ever, and I just have to have it. Pretty please with a cherry on top?" I said, making my best sad puppy dog face for my mom.

"I can't believe you are going to buy Freddy that game," said Suzie. "Just because he makes that face."

I turned to Suzie and whispered, "It works every time. Just watch." Then I turned back to my mom and made my eyes even bigger.

"Who said we're buying him the game?" said my dad.

"Please, please, please," I begged.

"It's not Christmas, and it's not your birthday, and thirty dollars is a lot of money. If you really want the game, then you'll have to pay for it with your own money," said my dad.

"My own money?! Really?"

"I guess that face doesn't work *every* time," Suzie whispered in my ear. "Nice try."

My dad nodded. "Yes, your own money."

I stuck out my lower lip and pouted. "But that's not fair!"

"Oh, it's very fair," said my dad. "We aren't going to buy you everything you want all the time. You get an allowance. If this is something you really want, then you'll buy it for yourself."

"May I please be excused?" I asked.

"You haven't even finished eating your dessert," said my mom. "Are you really going to leave mint chocolate chip ice cream sitting in your bowl? You usually lick the bowl clean."

I gobbled up the last few bites of my ice cream. It seemed a shame to waste my favorite flavor. "Now may I be excused?"

"Where are you going?" asked my dad. "I thought we were going to play catch."

"Up to my room. I need to see how much I have in my piggy bank!"

CHAPTER 4

Counting Money

I raced up the stairs into my bedroom and slammed the door behind me. I didn't want Suzie to see where I hid my piggy bank, and I definitely didn't want her to watch me count my money.

My piggy bank wasn't actually a pig at all. It was a shark. I got it one time when we went to the aquarium. I keep it hidden in the back of my underwear drawer because I know Suzie would never look in there.

I opened the drawer and felt around under the socks in the back for my bank. "Aha! Here

it is!" I said to myself as I pulled it out of my drawer. "I can't wait to see how much I've got."

I took the stopper out of the bottom of the bank and reached my hand in to pull out the bills. Then I shook it really hard so that the coins would fall out on the floor.

I had a handful of bills and a pile of change. "I sure hope I have thirty dollars here."

I started counting the bills first . . . five ones, two fives, and a ten. "Let's see—that's five, fifteen, twenty five. Cool! I already have twenty-five dollars right here in my hand. I just need five more dollars."

Just then my door flew open and Suzie barged into the room.

"Get out! Get out!" I yelled as I threw my body over my money to cover it up. "Don't you ever knock?"

"What are you doing?" asked Suzie.

"None of your beeswax. Now get out and leave me alone," I said.

"Are you counting your money?" said Suzie.

I just stared at her and pointed to the door.

"Do you need any help?"

"I don't need anything from you," I said. "I just need you to get out."

"Okay. Fine. I'm going," said Suzie as she walked out of my room.

"Hey, shut the door!" I called after her.

She pulled it closed and disappeared into her room.

Now she messed me up. I forgot how much I had

so far. I counted the bills again. "Oh, right. I have twenty-five dollars so far. I only need five more dollars."

I put the bills down and started sorting the pile of coins into pennies, nickels, dimes, and quarters. I figured it would be easier to count that way.

My heart was beating really fast. *Please be enough. Please be enough money to buy* Wonder World, I thought as I counted the coins.

I had three more dollars in quarters. That made twenty-eight dollars. "1 only need two more dollars. I bet I have that here," I said with a big grin on my face.

As I counted what was left in the pile, the smile started to fade from my face, and my heart sank. "No! No! This can't be possible," I said. I recounted the coins but got the same amount the second time.

I hit my fist on the floor. "I can't believe I'm a dollar short! I have twenty-nine dollars, and I need thirty!"

I sat back for a minute and hit my forehead with the palm of my hand. "Think, think, think."

Maybe I had left a dollar in one of my pockets. Once in a while I would find money I had forgotten about in my jacket pocket.

I ran over to my closet and started reaching into all of my coat pockets. I checked my winter coat, my raincoat, my sweatshirt jacket. Nothing! All of the pockets were empty.

I lay down on my bed. One dollar! All I needed was one dollar! Where was I going to get one dollar?

Just then I had an idea. "Suzie! Suzie!" I called.

No answer. I called again. "Suzie! Suzie!" Still nothing.

Of course when I don't want her around, she's always there, but when I actually need her for something, she's nowhere to be found.

"Ugh!" I sighed, and got up off my bed to go look for Suzie.

I opened my door and walked down the hall toward Suzie's room. She was lying on her bed, reading a book.

"Didn't you hear me calling you?" I asked.

"Yes, I did," said Suzie.

"So why didn't you answer me or come into my room?"

"You just told me to get out, and that you didn't need anything from me," said Suzie, "so why should I go running into your room?"

She could be so frustrating. Sometimes I wished I had a younger brother instead of an older sister, but right now I would have to be nice to her if I was going to get what I needed.

Suzie got up off her bed and started to gently push me toward the door. "You can leave now," she said.

I dug my heels into the carpet. "But I need to ask you something."

"What?" said Suzie. "What do you need to ask me?"

"I . . . umm . . . I . . . umm," I stammered.

"What is it? Spit it out already!"

I took a deep breath. "I need a dollar!" I blurted out.

Suzie didn't say anything. She just started laughing.

I stared at her and waited. "Well, aren't you going to say anything?"

"This is a joke, right?" said Suzie.

"No, it's not a joke. I really do need a dollar," I said.

"Why do you need a dollar?" asked Suzie.

"Well, I just counted all of the money in my piggy bank, and I have exactly twenty-nine dollars, but I need thirty dollars to buy *Wonder World*."

"So why don't you just wait until you get your next allowance, and then you'll have enough to buy it," said Suzie.

"I can't wait another week," I said.

"Why not?"

"Because I'll never be the first one to reach level ten if I don't start playing this week."

"Okay. Fine. I'll give you the dollar," said Suzie.

"Really?" I said, jumping up and down.

Just then Suzie held up her pinky for a pinky swear. "What's it worth to you?"

"Are you kidding?" I said.

Suzie just shook her head. "Did you really think I was just going to *give* you a dollar?"

"Ugh!" I groaned. "How about I do your chores tomorrow?"

"Tomorrow?" Suzie chuckled. "A dollar is worth way more than doing my chores for one day. I'll give you the dollar, but you have to do my chores for three days."

"Three days! You're crazy!" I said.

"Okay, then. No deal . . . no dollar," said Suzie, and she started to push me toward the door again.

"No! Wait, wait!" I said.

"I haven't got all night," said Suzie.

"Fine. I'll do your chores for three days," I said.

"So we have a deal?" said Suzie, holding up her pinky for a pinky swear.

"Yes, we have a deal," I said as we locked pinkies. "Now can I have the dollar?"

"I'll bring it to you in your room. I don't want you to see where I keep my piggy bank," said Suzie.

I walked back to my room, and a minute later Suzie was standing in the doorway with a dollar in her hand. "Here you go."

I grabbed it out of her hand and kissed it. Then I started dancing around my room, singing, "Now I got thirty . . . thirty dollars . . . Now I got thirty . . . thirty dollars . . ."

Suzie made the cuckoo sign by the side of her head and walked out.

CHAPTER 5

Let's Go, Go, Go!

"Mom, you have to take me to the mall after school today," I said at breakfast the next morning.

"Excuse me?" said my mom. "Are you giving me an order?"

"That's not a very polite way to speak to your mother," said my dad.

"You're right. Sorry, Mom," I said.

"Why don't you try that again?" my dad said.

"Mom, do you think you might be able to take me to the mall after school today?"

"That sounded much better," said my mom. "Yes, I think we probably have time to go to the mall. Why do you want to go? Do you need to get something for school?"

"He just wants to buy that dumb video game," said Suzie.

"It's not a dumb game," I said. "I really need it."

"But I thought you said it cost thirty dollars," said my dad.

"It does!"

"I told you we're not going to buy it for you."

"I know. I dumped out my piggy bank last night and counted all of my money," I said. "I have just enough to buy it."

"You've saved up thirty dollars?" said my dad. "Where did you get all that money?"

"Some of it is my allowance, some of it is birthday money, and some of it I got for walking Baxter for Mrs. Golden."

"Wow! I'm impressed," said my mom. "Good for you."

"So do you think we can go when I get home from school?"

"Sorry, but you can't go today," said Suzie.

I whipped my head around. "Yes I can."

"No you can't."

"Yes I can!"

"No you can't!"

"Well, you're not the boss of me!" I shouted.

"All right, that's enough, you two," said my dad. "If you keep arguing, then no one is going to the mall."

"Suzie, why are you saying that Freddy can't go to the mall?" asked my mom.

"Because you have to take Kimberly and me to ballet class today. It's your turn to drive the car pool."

"That's no big deal," said my mom. "I can drop you girls off at ballet, Freddy and I can run over to the mall, and then we'll come back to pick you up."

"Kids at school keep talking about how they have to wait in really long lines to buy that

game," said Suzie. "My ballet class is only an hour long."

"I don't think we'll be standing in line that long," my mom said, laughing. "Don't worry, we'll be back on time."

I wasn't going to tell her that some kids had even waited three hours in line to buy the game. She'd never take me.

"So we're all set? You can take me today for sure?" I asked my mom.

She nodded.

"Promise?"

"Yes, Freddy, I promise," said my mom.

"Great! See you after school!" I said as I grabbed my backpack and dashed out the door to catch the bus.

I couldn't think about anything else all day except buying that game. I didn't think that school was ever going to end. Time seemed to move in slow motion.

When the bus dropped me off at home, I threw open my front door and yelled, "Mom! I'm home! Let's go, go, go! It's *Wonder World* time!"

I heard my mom's voice from the back of the house. "Freddy, I'm in the laundry room."

I ran back to the laundry room and found my mom taking clothes out of the dryer. "Here you go," she said, handing me a big pile of laundry.

"What's this?" I said.

"It's your laundry, silly," said my mom.

"But you promised you'd take me to the mall today to get the video game. Remember?"

"Of course I remember," said my mom. "But first you need to fold your clean laundry."

"Can't I just do it when we get home?" I asked. "The store only gets a few copies of the game each day, and I don't want them to sell out."

"Then you'd better hurry up and start folding," my mom said, smiling, "because your chores come first. We're not going to the mall until all of your laundry is folded and put away."

I scooped up all of my clothes, raced upstairs to my room, and quickly folded everything and put it away.

"Ready, Mom!" I called from my room. "All done!"

"No you're not," said a voice from behind me.

I turned around to find Suzie standing in my room with a big pile of clothes in her hands.

"Get out!" I yelled.

Suzie walked over and dumped her pile of clothes on my bed.

I picked up a pair of her underwear and threw it at her. "Get this stuff out of here!" I shouted.

"I will as soon as you fold it," she said, smiling.

"Are you crazy? I'm not folding your stinky clothes!"

"Oh, yes you are. Last night when you asked me for that dollar, we made a deal. You swore you would do my chores for three days. Well, folding laundry is one of my chores, so start folding," said Suzie, and she walked out of the room.

If I didn't fold her clothes, then she would take the dollar back, and I wouldn't have enough money to buy the game. I didn't really have a choice. I had to fold her laundry.

I got all of Suzie's clothes folded and put away, and then I bounded down the stairs into the kitchen. "All set!" I said. "Everything is folded and put away."

"Everything?" Suzie asked. "Are you sure you folded everything?"

"Yes, I'm sure," I answered, glaring at her. "It's all done."

"Then I guess we can get going," said my

mom. "We just have to pick up Kimberly on the way. Do you have your money, Freddy?"

"Oops! I forgot," I said, laughing. "Good thing you reminded me."

I leaped up the stairs two at a time, shoved my money in my pocket, and raced back down. "Now I'm really ready!" I said with a big smile on my face. "Let's go, go, go!"

"Calm down," said Suzie. "I don't want you to embarrass me in front of Kimberly."

"I'm just so excited," I said, jumping up and down. "I can't wait to get this game!"

We drove over to Kimberly's house to pick her up, and she sat down next to me in the car. I couldn't stop bouncing around in my seat.

"What's his problem?" Kimberly asked Suzie. "Why is he acting so weird?"

"You mean weirder than usual?" said Suzie. "He's going to get that new video game *Wonder World*."

"Oh," said Kimberly. "Robbie can't stop

talking about that game, and he plays it all the time. That's all he does."

"I know!" I said. "It's so cool. Robbie was showing me how to play it the other day at Josh's house."

"I think Robbie just got to level four," said Kimberly.

Level four! There was no time to waste. I had to get this game, and fast!

CHAPTER 6

Got It!

We dropped the girls off at ballet and drove over to the mall. As soon as we got inside the doors, I took off running.

"Freddy, slow down! Wait for me!" my mom called, jogging after me. "You need to walk."

"Hurry up, Mom," I yelled over my shoulder. "We don't have a lot of time!"

When we got to the Game Place, the line was out the door. "Oh no!" I cried. "There are so many people!"

"It's not a big deal," said my mom. "If we run

out of time today, we can always come back tomorrow."

"No, I have to get it *today*," I whined.

"Then you'd better get in line," said my mom.

We got in line and waited, and waited, and waited. Every two minutes I asked my mom what time it was. The line seemed to crawl as slowly as a snail. I was so nervous I kept biting my nails.

"If we don't get up there in the next ten minutes, then we'll need to come back tomorrow," said my mom. "I can't be late to pick up the girls."

"But I can't leave without it," I said. "I just have to get it."

"Sorry, honey," said my mom. "That's just the way it is."

"Come on, come on," I mumbled under my breath. "Let's go." There were still three people ahead of me in line, and it didn't look like they had too many copies left. I rubbed my shark's tooth for good luck.

With one minute to go, I finally reached the front of the line.

"How can I help you?" asked the guy at the cash register.

"I'd like the new game *Wonder World*, please," I said.

"Wow! You're in luck," the guy said, handing me the game. "This is the last one I have. Everyone else is going to have to come back tomorrow."

Whew! I sighed with relief and patted my lucky shark's tooth.

"Thanks a lot!" I said as I handed the guy my money. "I can't wait to play it."

"It's a lot of fun!" he said.

"What level are you on?" I asked him.

"Level six."

"Six? Wow! That's amazing."

"Well, good luck," he said as he handed me the game.

"Thanks!" I said again. I grabbed the game and left the store.

"That was lucky," said my mom.

I didn't answer. I was too busy looking at the game in my hands.

"Freddy, I'm talking to you," said my mom.

I still didn't answer.

My mom tapped gently on my head. "Hello, is anybody in there?"

"Huh? What? Oh, sorry, Mom. What did you say?"

"I said that was lucky. We made it in time, and you got the last one."

"Really lucky," I said with a giant grin on my face.

As soon as we got home, I tore open the game and started playing. I didn't realize how long I had been playing until my mom called me for dinner.

"Freddy! Freddy! Where are you?" said my mom.

"I'm in the den!" I shouted.

My mom walked in. "Why didn't you answer me? I called you three times already for dinner."

"Sorry, Mom!" I said. "I didn't hear you."

"Well, it's dinnertime. You need to turn that thing off and go wash your hands."

"I'll be there in a minute. I just have to—"

"No, you'll turn it off now, or I'm going to take it away. Dinner is getting cold."

My mom stood there. She wasn't going to leave until I turned off the game. I saved what I had done so far, so I could continue after dinner, and went to wash my hands.

When I sat down at the table, my dad said, "What did you do today, kids?"

"I practiced a new dance for my ballet recital," said Suzie.

"That's wonderful!" said my dad. "I can't wait for your recital. I always love watching you dance. And how about you, Freddy? What did you do? Did you practice playing catch with Josh and Robbie?"

"No, I didn't have time to play catch. Mom took me to the mall to get that new video game *Wonder World*."

"Oh, that's right," said my dad. "Have you tried it yet?"

"Tried it?" said Suzie. "That's all he's done since he got home. He's been sitting in front of that TV for two hours!"

"Two hours! You must really like that game."

"It's awesome! I got my house built, and I was searching for the treasure in level one when an Evil Serpent appeared out of nowhere and lunged at me like this," I said as I jumped up out of my chair and lunged at Suzie.

I guess I startled Suzie because she screamed, bumped into the table, and accidentally spilled her glass of milk.

"Now look what you made me do!" she shouted. The milk was trickling off the table and making a puddle on her chair.

"Freddy," said my mom. "What do you say to your sister?"

"Sorry, Suzie," I said.

"Now go get some paper towels to clean up this mess," said my mom.

I wiped up the floor and Suzie's chair and sat back down.

Suzie gave me the evil eye from across the table. She looked really mad.

I looked down at my plate and started shoveling forkfuls of spaghetti into my mouth.

"Whoa, whoa, slow down there," said my dad. "You're going to choke."

"No I'm not," I said with a mouthful of food.

"Ewww! You're disgusting," said Suzie. "You have little pieces of spaghetti falling out of your mouth."

"Freddy, you know it's not polite to talk with your mouth full," said my mom. "You need to chew up your food and then you can talk."

"Slow down," said my dad. "What's the rush?"

"I need go play some more *Wonder World*. I haven't even gotten past level one yet, and Kimberly said today that Robbie is already on level four! May I please be excused?"

"No," said my dad.

"Why not?"

"Because it's dinnertime. You don't play video games during dinner."

"And after dinner, you have to take a shower," said my mom.

"Can I skip the shower tonight?" I said, lifting up my T-shirt to smell it. "I don't smell bad."

"Freddy!" said my mom. "Stop smelling yourself at the table. You are taking a shower. It's not a choice."

"And after your shower, you have to do your homework," said Suzie.

"Like I said this morning, you're not the boss of me," I mumbled.

"Your sister is right," said my dad. "No more video games until you finish your homework."

"But . . ."

"No buts," said my dad. "School is more important than a video game."

"But I have to play more tonight. I just have to!"

CHAPTER 7

Gotta Play

I took the fastest shower ever and sat down to do my homework.

"Do you need any help, honey?" my mom asked.

"No thanks. I just have to do a few math problems and practice my spelling words."

I tried my hardest to stay focused, so I could get done quickly and go back to playing *Wonder World*. After about a half hour, I was finished.

"Done!" I announced.

"No you're not," said Suzie.

"Yes I am. I did my math and my spelling. I don't have anything else tonight."

"You haven't done your reading for your reading log yet."

"I'll just do that later when I get in bed," I said.

"No, like your father said at dinner: School is more important," said my mom. "You need to do your reading before you play video games."

"Awwww, Mom, pleeeaase? Just this once," I begged. "I promise I'll do it later. I really have to get past level one in *Wonder World* before tomorrow."

"Sorry, Freddy, but you need to do your reading now," said my mom.

I stuck my tongue out at Suzie when my mom wasn't looking and mouthed the words, "Thanks a lot." Then I grabbed my book and stomped up the stairs to my room.

As soon as I finished my reading, I raced back downstairs to start playing *Wonder World*.

"Oh, Freddy. I see you are all done with your homework. That's great," said my mom. "You still have time to play your game."

"What time is it?" I asked.

"It's seven thirty. You have a half hour to play."

"A half hour! I can't do anything in a half hour! I won't even get past level one," I said, pouting.

"You're wasting your time by complaining," said my mom.

I quickly turned on the game, but the half hour passed by way too quickly, and soon I had to turn it off and go to bed.

As I lay in my bed, I realized that I couldn't tell everyone at school tomorrow that I hadn't even made it past level one. That would be too embarrassing. Then I remembered Josh told me he had gotten up at five o'clock in the morning to play. That's exactly what I should do. I would get up really early before school started and play some more.

Riiinnng, riiinnng, riiinnng. My alarm clock screamed in my ear. I smacked the button to turn it off and rubbed my eyes. It was still dark outside. I was about to pull the covers back over my head, when I remembered why I had set the alarm in the first place. *Wonder World*! I had to get up now and try to get past level one before school today.

I quietly opened my bedroom door and peeked out in the hall. The coast was clear. Everyone else was still asleep.

I tiptoed down the stairs, making sure I skipped the step that always creaked. My mom had supersonic hearing, and if she knew I was up this early just to play a video game, she'd make me go back to bed.

I started the game and turned the volume way down, so no one would hear me. I got so involved in playing that I didn't realize two hours had passed and the sun was up.

"Freddy?"

My mom's voice startled me, and I jumped about three feet off the couch. "Mom! You scared me!"

"Sorry, honey. What are you doing?"

"Playing *Wonder World*."

"How long have you been down here? What time did you get up?"

"I'm not sure," I said.

"Well, you need to turn that off and get ready for school," said my mom. "I don't want you to miss the bus."

"All right, Mom. Give me one more minute," I said. "I have to save what I've done before I turn it off."

I had managed to finish level one. All of my friends were so far ahead of me. I wished it were a Saturday, so I could just keep playing. I knew I could catch up to Robbie and Josh if I had more time to play. I was starting to get the hang of it.

When I got on the bus, everyone was talking about *Wonder World*.

"Did you get the game yesterday?" asked Josh.

"Yes, I did," I said with a big smile on my face.

"Kimberly told me you got the last one in the store," said Robbie.

"Yep. I was so lucky," I said.

"That's awesome," said Josh. "Did you start playing?"

"I started yesterday, but I didn't get very far because I kept getting attacked by the Evil Serpents!"

"They are sneaky," said Josh. "You really have to watch out for them."

"I actually got up before school this morning to play some more."

"You got up early?" said Robbie. "You never get up early."

"I know," I said, laughing, "but I just had to try to get past level one."

Just then Max, the biggest bully in the whole second grade, turned around in his seat. "Level one? Did you just say you're on level one?"

I nodded my head.

"Hey, everybody, Freddy is only on level one in *Wonder World*," Max announced to the whole bus.

I turned bright red and slid down in my seat. I was so embarrassed.

"*He's* probably only on level one," I whispered to Robbie and Josh.

Max leaned over the seat and grabbed me by my shirt. "What did you say, Sharkbreath?"

"I . . . uhhh . . . I . . . uhhh . . . I said he's probably having fun."

Max glared at me and tightened his grip on my shirt. "That's not what you said," he growled.

"Let go of Freddy!" said Josh.

"Why should I?" said Max.

"Because I said so," Josh said, grabbing Max's hand and pulling it off my shirt. "What level are you on, Big Mouth? You probably haven't even made it past level one."

"Yes, I have!" said Max. "I have made it to level six."

"Six?" Robbie whispered to me. "Max is on level six?"

"I don't believe you," said Josh. "Prove it."

"How am I going to prove it?" said Max. "You want to come to my house after school and see it with your own eyes?"

That was the last thing Josh wanted to do. "No thanks," said Josh. "I know how you can prove it. Tell me what the treasure is for level five. If you've made it to level six, then you found the treasure in level five."

"Oooo, good one," Robbie whispered. "He's got Max now."

"Ummm . . . ummm," Max stammered.

"I knew it!" said Josh. "You haven't gotten to level six."

"The level five treasure is the sparkling sapphire," Max blurted out.

Josh stared at Max for a minute without saying anything.

"Is he right?" I whispered to Robbie.

Robbie nodded.

"Wow! You are telling the truth," said Josh. "Congratulations on getting to level six, but I'm still going to be the first one to reach level ten."

"No you're not," said Max. "I'm going to be the first one to reach level ten. No one is going to beat me."

"We'll see about that," said Josh.

Yeah, we'll see about that, I thought to myself.

CHAPTER 8

Level Ten

I was obsessed with playing *Wonder World*. I played it all day, every day, for a week. I didn't do anything else. I just had to be the first person to reach level ten.

One morning, after getting up early to play, I heard my mom calling, "Freddy! Freddy! Hurry up! Time for breakfast!"

I dragged myself into the kitchen. I could barely keep my eyes open.

"Are you all right, honey?" said my mom.

I yawned a big yawn and lay my head down on the kitchen table.

"You look exhausted," said my dad.

"It's because he keeps getting up early to play that dumb video game," said Suzie.

"It's not dumb," I mumbled.

"You are playing it way too much," said my mom. "It's not healthy."

"When was the last time you went outside to play with your friends?" asked my dad.

I shrugged my shoulders. "I don't know."

"I think you should stop playing it for a while and go play catch with your friends after school today."

"I can't."

"Why not? You need to get ready for Little League," said my dad.

"But if I stop playing, then I won't be the first person to get to level ten!" I said.

"So?" said my mom.

"Ugh!" I groaned. "You just don't get it."

"Well, you need to sit up and eat some breakfast," said my mom. "Here. I already put cream cheese on your bagel for you."

I tried sitting up in my chair, but I was so tired that I was having a hard time holding my head up.

I took a bite of bagel and chewed it slowly.

"Look at you, Freddy," said my mom. "You look half asleep. You're chewing with your eyes closed!"

Just as she said that, my head fell forward into my plate.

"AAAHHH! Oh my goodness!" my mom yelled.

Her scream startled me, and I sat up with a jolt. "Huh? What?"

Suzie was pointing at me and laughing hysterically. "Ha, ha, ha, ha, ha!"

"What? What's so funny?"

"You've got cream cheese all over your face," said Suzie. "You look like you went to the beauty parlor and got a face mask."

My mom ran to the sink to get a paper towel to wipe off my face. "What a mess! That's it, Freddy! No more getting up early to play that silly game."

"But I have to, Mom. I just have to," I said.

"No, your mother is right," said my dad. "You have gotten too obsessed with that game. It has taken over your life!"

"You're so tired that you're falling asleep at the breakfast table," said my mom.

"I think we're going to put a limit on how much you can play each day," said my dad.

"Good idea," said Suzie.

I turned to Suzie. "No one asked you," I said.

"You can play for one hour each day, and that's it," said my mom.

"One hour a day! I'll never be the first one to get to level ten now."

"I don't care," said my mom. "You need to get outside and breathe some fresh air."

I crossed my arms and stuck out my lower lip.

"Pouting is going to get you nowhere," said my mom.

Just then I heard the bus brakes screech to a halt.

"Now look! The bus is already here, and you haven't eaten any breakfast," said my mom. "Here, take this with you," she said, shoving a granola bar and a cheese stick into my hand.

I tried to run to catch the bus, but I just didn't have the energy. I stumbled on my way up the steps and tripped.

Max, of course, was pointing and

laughing at me. "Ha, ha, ha! Freddy, did you have a nice trip?"

"Very funny," I mumbled as I made my way back to my seat.

"You look awful," said Robbie.

"Thanks," I said.

"Are you okay, Freddy?" asked Josh. "What's wrong?"

I opened my mouth wide and yawned a huge yawn. "I'm just really tired. That's all."

"Why are you so tired?" said Robbie.

"Because I keep getting up really early every morning to play *Wonder World*."

"Did you just say *Wonder World*?" said Max.

Oh no. Here we go again, I thought to myself.

"What level are you on now, little baby? Level two?"

I scowled at Max, but I didn't say anything.

"You think you're such a big shot," Josh said to Max, "but I have news for you."

"Oh really?" said Max. "I can't wait to hear it."

"I have gotten to level nine," said Josh.

"Way to go!" I said, giving Josh a high five.

"I bet you by tomorrow, I will be the first person to reach level ten," Josh said, poking his finger into Max's chest.

Max stared at Josh. I wasn't sure what he was going to do.

"Too bad. So sad," said Max.

"What are you talking about?" said Josh.

"I just reached level ten this morning," said Max, grinning from ear to ear.

"No way!"

"Yes way! I gave the Wizard of Wonder World all ten enchanted treasures, and now I have been crowned king."

I gasped.

"Did he just say he was crowned king?" Robbie whispered.

I nodded. "Uh-huh."

"Well, congratulations, Max," said Josh.

"I am the king!" Max shouted, and he pounded himself on the chest.

"I can't believe it," I said.

"Me either," said Robbie.

"We spent all of that time playing *Wonder World*, and in the end Max beat all of us," Josh said.

"You know what, guys?" I said.

"What?" Robbie and Josh said together.

"I really missed playing with you guys this past week."

"I did, too," said Robbie.

"Me, too," said Josh.

"You're my best friends, and I didn't see you all week," I said.

"Let's get together after school today," said Josh.

"We could go bug hunting," said Robbie.

"Or play catch," said Josh.

"I don't care what we do, as long as we're together," I said, smiling.

Then we all gave each other a high five.

Freddy's Fun
Pages

MAGIC LETTER SCRAMBLE

Can you come up with ten words using the letters in *VIDEO GAME*?
(You can only use each letter once in a word except for the letter "e." You may use the "e" twice.)
Example: MADE

1. _____

2. _____

3. _____

4. _____

5. _____

6. _____

7. _____

8. _____

9. _____

10. _____

BE AN ILLUSTRATOR!

What do you think these characters
from *Wonder World* look like?

Wizard of Wonder World	Ariana
Triglops	Evil Serpent

WIZARD JOKES

Share these funny wizard jokes with your friends. Just make sure there are no wizards around to hear you, or they might put a spell on you!

What do you call a wizard from outer space?
A flying sorcerer!

Why do wizards brush their teeth three times a day?
To prevent bat breath!

How do you talk to an angry wizard?
Very carefully.

What do you get if you cross a wizard with an iceberg?

A cold spell.

What happened when the wizard met the witch?

It was love at first fright!